Thomas Nast

Thomas Nast's Christmas Drawings for the Human Race

Thomas Nast

Thomas Nast's Christmas Drawings for the Human Race

ISBN/EAN: 9783337412371

Printed in Europe, USA, Canada, Australia, Japan

Cover: Foto ©Andreas Hilbeck / pixelio.de

More available books at **www.hansebooks.com**

Thomas Nast's
CHRISTMAS DRAWINGS

FOR

THE HUMAN RACE

NEW YORK   HARPER & BROTHERS   PRINTERS &
PUBLISHERS   FRANKLIN SQUARE   M DCCC XC

PUBLISHER'S NOTE.

THIS volume of Mr. Nast's "Christmas Drawings" is the first collection of his works which has been published. The pictures are well called "Drawings for the Human Race," because they appeal to the sympathy of no particular religious denomination or political party, but to the universal delight in the happiest of holidays, consecrated by the loftiest associations and endeared by the tenderest domestic traditions. Christmas is the holiday of all; but it is especially the Children's day. The grotesque and airy fancies of childhood which cling about Santa Claus, as the good genius of Christmas, are reproduced upon these pages, in delightfully imaginative reality by the sympathetic touch of the artist, so that the book is an overflowing feast of true Christmas cheer.

Mr. Nast's hand, when dealing with current topics of the time, tips the flashing shafts of wit with morality; with relentless humor puts cunning pretence in the pillory; and exposes public wrong to the fatal merriment which laughs it away. But the artist's hand is never happier than when, with the lambent light of the same humor, it irradiates the play of domestic affection, and makes the home circle gay. It is the bluff, honest Santa Claus of " The Night before Christmas ;" the Santa Claus of the reindeer and the sleigh, alighting on the snowy roof, and descending the chimney with his wondrous pack of treasures; the Santa Claus of unsuspecting childhood, and the Mother Goose of undoubting infancy, to whom these pages introduce us. There is no child who cannot understand them, no parent who cannot enjoy them. Mr. Nast is fairly without a rival in this kind. His Santa Claus is old Father Christmas himself, and his welcome will be as general and as hearty as that which salutes the crammed and enchanted stocking on Christmas morning.

STOCKING OF CONTENTS.

SANTA CLAUS.

Th. Nast.

MERRY
CHRISTMAS

SANTA CLAUS'S ROUTE.

DARNING THE STOCKINGS.

"WHO SAID ANYTHING ABOUT CHRISTMAS DINNER?"

CHRISTMAS GREENS.

"So now is come our joyful'st feast—   Each room with ivy leaves is cheer'd,
Let every man be jolly ;   And every post with holly."

CHRISTMAS POST.

SANTA CLAUS'S MAIL.

"HELLO! SANTA CLAUS!"

"HELLO! LITTLE ONE!"

"'TWAS THE NIGHT BEFORE CHRISTMAS."

A chance to test Santa Claus's generosity.

MESSAGES AND LISTS FOR SANTA CLAUS.

RECIPROCATION.

"Won't Santa Claus be surprised to find that he has not been forgotten?"

"He prayed, 'And let Santa Claus fill my stockings just as full as he can. Amen.'"

THE WATCH ON CHRISTMAS EVE.

CHRISTMAS EVE.—Santa Claus waiting for the children to get to sleep.

SEEING SANTA CLAUS.

A VERY BAD BOY.

"'Twas the night before Christmas, and all through the house
Not a creature was stirring, *not even a mouse.*"

CHRISTMAS STATION.

RINGING IN THE AIR.

DING! DONG!!

CHRISTMAS EVE.—OLD FACES FOR YOUNG HEARTS.

MERRY CHRISTMAS.

A CHRISTMAS SKETCH.—"Five o'clock in the morning."

CAUGHT!

THE SHRINE OF ST. NICHOLAS.—"We are all good children."

"Little Bo-Peep fell fast asleep, and dreampt—"

SEE! THE CHRISTMAS PLUM PUDDING.

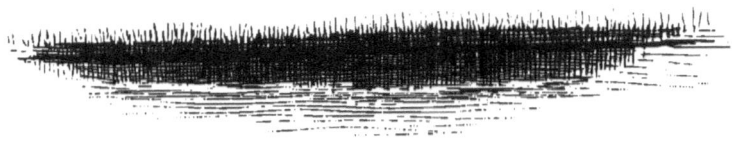

"COME NOW, SANTA CLAUS, I'S READY."

CHRISTKINDCHEN.

CHRISTMAS FLIRTATION.

CHRISTMAS FLIRTATION.

THE DOMESTIC EXPRESS.

Old Bachelor: "How glad I am that I don't have to cart round endless bundles for greedy brats during the holidays."

NURSERY TILES.—"There he is."

THE CRUSTY OLD BACHELOR WHO IS BOUND TO HAVE SOMETHING IN HIS STOCKING.

A CHRISTMAS STORY.—"I am Cinderella, and you are the wicked sisters."

MERRY OLD SANTA CLAUS.

SANTA CLAUS'S REBUKE.

"I'll never do it again."

THE CHRIST CHILD.

THE DEAR LITTLE BOY THAT THOUGHT CHRISTMAS CAME OFTENER.

MOVING DAY.

"For he's a jolly good fellow, so say we all of us."

SANTA CLAUS'S TOOL-BOX.

CHRISTMAS IN CAMP.

A MERRY CHRISTMAS.

"Merry Christmas to all, and to all a good-night."

"Wishing you a Merry Christmas and a Happy New Year."

'TWAS THE NIGHT AFTER CHRISTMAS.

www.ingramcontent.com/pod-product-compliance
Lightning Source LLC
Chambersburg PA
CBHW032014010726

47493CB00007B/2394